Agatha
Girl of Mystery

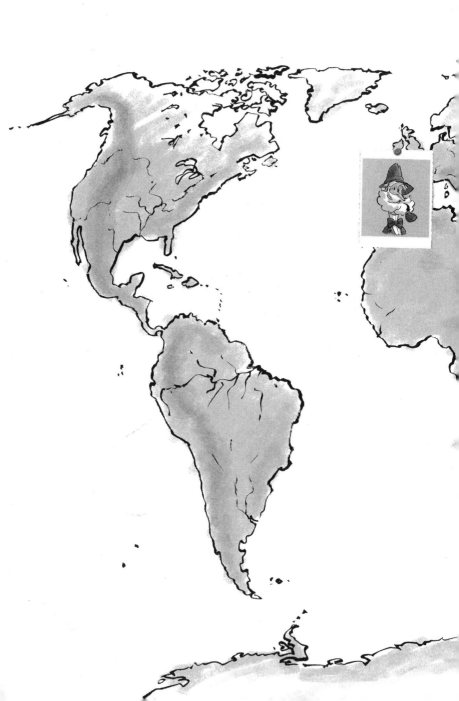

GROSSET & DUNLAP
Published by the Penguin Group
Penguin Group (USA) Inc., 375 Hudson Street, New York, New York 10014, USA
Penguin Group (Canada), 90 Eglinton Avenue East, Suite 700, Toronto, Ontario M4P 2Y3, Canada
(a division of Pearson Penguin Canada Inc.)
Penguin Books Ltd, 80 Strand, London WC2R 0RL, England
Penguin Ireland, 25 St Stephen's Green, Dublin 2, Ireland (a division of Penguin Books Ltd)
Penguin Group (Australia), 707 Collins Street, Melbourne, Victoria 3008, Australia
(a division of Pearson Australia Group Pty Ltd)
Penguin Books India Pvt Ltd, 11 Community Centre, Panchsheel Park, New Delhi–110 017, India
Penguin Group (NZ), 67 Apollo Drive, Rosedale, Auckland 0632, New Zealand
(a division of Pearson New Zealand Ltd)
Penguin Books (South Africa), Rosebank Office Park, 181 Jan Smuts Avenue, Parktown North 2193, South Africa
Penguin China, B7 Jiaming Center, 27 East Third Ring Road North, Chaoyang District, Beijing 100020, China

Penguin Books Ltd, Registered Offices: 80 Strand, London WC2R 0RL, England

Original Title: Agatha Mistery: La spada del re di Scozia
Text by Sir Steve Stevenson
Original cover and illustrations by Stefano Turconi

English language edition copyright © 2013 Penguin Group (USA) Inc. Original edition published by Istituto
Geografico De Agostini S.p.A., Italy, 2010. © 2010 Atlantyca Dreamfarm s.r.l., Italy

International Rights © Atlantyca S.p.A.–via Leopardi 8, 20123 Milano, Italia
foreignrights@atlantyca.it–www.atlantyca.com

Published in 2013 by Grosset & Dunlap, a division of Penguin Young Readers Group, 345 Hudson Street,
New York, New York 10014. GROSSET & DUNLAP is a trademark of Penguin Group (USA) Inc. Printed in the U.S.A.

Library of Congress Cataloging-in-Publication Data is available.

10 9 8 7 6 5 4 3 2 1

ISBN 978-0-448-46220-2

PEARSON

ALWAYS LEARNING

ha

Girl of Mystery

The King of Scotland's Sword

by Sir Steve Stevenson
illustrated by Stefano Turconi

translated by Siobhan Tracey
adapted by Maya Gold

Grosset & Dunlap
An Imprint of Penguin Group (USA) Inc.

THIRD MISSION
Agents

Agatha
Twelve years old, an
aspiring mystery writer;
has a formidable memory

Dash
Agatha's cousin and student
at the private school Eye
International Detective Academy

Chandler
Butler and former boxer with impeccable British style

Watson
Obnoxious Siberian cat with the nose of a bloodhound

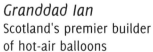

Granddad Ian
Scotland's premier builder of hot-air balloons

DESTINATION

Scotland:
Dunnottar Castle, Aberdeen
Edinburgh
Bowden

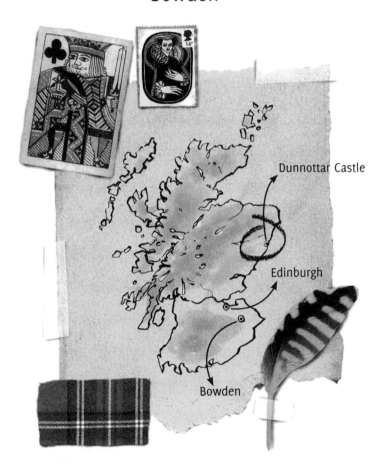

Dunnottar Castle

Edinburgh

Bowden

OBJECTIVE

To discover who stole the
ancient broadsword that once
belonged to the legendary king
of Scotland Robert the Bruce.

The Investigation Begins...

$\mathcal{L}$ondoners are famous for staying up late, and Dash Mistery was a total night owl. But the fresh air of Scotland, combined with a very big dinner, made him doze off at nine. One minute he was sprawled on the living-room couch with a plaid blanket over his knees, listening to his granddad Ian and younger cousin Agatha as they sat by a crackling fire, trading stories of their adventures in faraway places. The next, he was out like a light. Was he dreaming, or did somebody lift him up gently and carry him into his bedroom, the way his mom used to when he was a kid?

Dash opened his eyes at 7:00 the next morning. The room was eerily silent. Where were his seven computers and the hip-hop mix he always woke up to? For a moment, he had no clue where he was. Then he saw the emerald hills outside the window, crisscrossed with ancient stone walls, and it all flooded back. He was in his grandfather's country house on the outskirts of Edinburgh, the capital of Scotland, where the Mistery family was gathering for their traditional hot-air-balloon weekend. There was no time to lose!

He and Agatha were to join Granddad Ian at noon for a balloon flight over the Scottish Highlands. But before they took off, he had a chore to get out of the way. Dash was already sorry he'd let himself get roped into it.

"Childhood friends are a pain in the butt," he groaned, rolling over in bed. It would be easy to just go back to sleep. Instead, he kicked off his

five layers of wool blankets, like a deep-sea diver coming up for air.

He yawned and stretched, padding into the bathroom. He reached for the hair gel he always used to sculpt his floppy hair into a work of art, then paused in mid-motion. *No London style around here,* he said to himself with a grin. *If I go to meet Aileen looking like a total slob, maybe she'll quit stalking me with all those texts full of little hearts!*

Aileen Ferguson was fourteen years old, the same age as Dash. Her parents had sent her to a fancy boarding school in Edinburgh, but she was spending the weekend in the little Scottish town of Bowden, where Granddad Ian lived. As soon as she'd heard Dash was coming, she'd insisted on catching up with her old friend. "Okay, make it Saturday morning," Dash had finally agreed. "I'll meet you for breakfast, but I'm warning you, I'll have to leave in a hurry."

Dash rummaged through bureau drawers

until he found a heavy wool sweater that looked like the side of a sheep. He pulled on a pair of stiff corduroy pants and tucked them into a pair of bright green rubber boots. He looked at himself in the mirror. "I look like I fell off a haystack." He grinned. "I bet this is the last time Aileen will ever want to lay eyes on me!"

Dash had met Aileen several summers ago, when he spent a few weeks with his granddad. Everyone in Bowden called her "Dorothy" because she always wore a blue-checkered pinafore with red shoes, and tied her two pigtails

with ribbons, like the girl in *The Wizard of Oz*.

Dash checked the time on his EyeNet, a high-tech gadget that doubled as cell phone, computer, and anything else a budding detective might need in the field. It was almost 8:00. *And if everything goes well, I'll be a free man by ten!* he told himself.

He scrawled a quick note on the message board next to the door, then went outside and grabbed his bike. Within a few minutes, he was weaving along winding roads through the green Scottish countryside. There were thistles and heather and even a few grazing sheep. He

soon arrived in the village of Bowden, passing an ancient stone church and a line of pastel Georgian houses. There weren't many people out this early on a Saturday morning, and the inn where Aileen had arranged for them to meet looked completely deserted.

Dash entered boldly and strode right up to the counter.

The innkeeper wore a chef's hat and a dish towel over one shoulder as he rolled out dough for a tart. "Young Mr. Mistery?" he asked without turning around.

Dash paused, dumbfounded. "Uh yeah, that's me," he stammered. "How did you know?"

"Table six, in the corner," the man replied, picking up a knife to slice some pears.

Dash looked around the elegant dining room, wondering why Aileen had booked a table for two in the corner. Was she trying to create a romantic atmosphere?

He sat down with a sigh and waited.

The innkeeper came over, lit the candle in the center of the lace tablecloth, and walked away without a word.

Dash gave another sigh, even deeper this time.

Suddenly the door swung open. A slender girl stood on the threshold, sun striking her light brown hair. She had bright green eyes and the face of an angel, and was wearing a dress that any girl in London would have called cool. In short, she was gorgeous. And she was walking right toward him!

"Hi, Dash," the girl greeted him with a perfect smile. "Sorry I'm late."

The young detective could feel himself blushing. "Uh, oh, hi,

Dorothy," he managed to say. Embarrassed, he tried to correct himself. "I mean, Aileen."

She sat down at the table. "I like your look. Very retro, you know?" she said with a smile as she picked up her menu. "You look like an old-school Scotsman!"

Dash caught a glimpse of his reflection in the window and felt a sinking shame. Could he be any more of a loser? The annoying little girl he remembered had grown up to be totally cool. How was he going to catch up? He decided the best way to impress Aileen was to show off his EyeNet. It usually left people openmouthed, asking where they could get one. The answer, of course, was that they were only available to students of Eye International Detective Academy, but Dash's plans to become the world's greatest detective were definitely a secret.

"Hey, check out my new cell phone," he said slyly, pushing the EyeNet onto the table. "It's

a brand-new prototype, not on the market yet!" He readied himself to respond to a thousand questions, but Aileen barely glanced at it.

"Want to try the vegetarian haggis?" she asked, fixing him with a magnetic stare.

It was hard to imagine a worse combination than tofu and the traditional Scottish pudding made of organ meats, oatmeal, suet, and spices. Dash muttered a few words in response. Luckily just at that moment, the EyeNet gave a shrill beep. Like lightning, he grabbed it to look at the screen, which was flashing CODE RED.

It was a message from Eye International.

An urgent mission!

Dash jolted out of his seat. "Right now?" he blurted, realizing he had to get back to Agatha as soon as possible. She was the only one who could help him with an urgent investigation. He stared helplessly at Aileen. He would so much rather stay with her a little bit longer . . . She was awesome!

But duty was duty. Dash let out a big sigh and muttered, "Uh, um, excuse me, Dorothy, I've got to go. It's superimportant . . . I'll call you as soon as I'm finished, I promise!" He blushed again. "I meant, *Aileen.* Sorry, Dorothy!"

Feeling like a fool, he rushed out the door.

Aileen watched him get back on his bicycle and speed away, then gave a long sigh of her own. To console herself, she ordered a fruit salad with whipped cream and hot fudge sauce. "You know something, Mr. MacGaylin?" she said to the silent innkeeper. "There are easier things than having a crush on a wack job like Dashiell Mistery!"

CHAPTER ONE

Change of Plans

*A*spiring detective Dash Mistery was far from the wackiest branch on his family tree. For generations, the Misteries had dedicated themselves to unusual jobs: camel wranglers, underwater photographers, intercontinental explorers, truffle tasters in fancy restaurants, experts on prehistoric butterflies, custodians of remote islands, restorers of garden gnomes . . . The list went on and on.

No two Misteries were alike!

The previous evening, while Dash lay snoring under his tartan blanket, Agatha and Granddad Ian had laughed themselves silly at their relatives' bizarre professions. "You're the first mystery writer in the clan, dear Agatha," Granddad Ian had observed as he rose from his armchair to add another log to the fire. The living room was filled with the sweet smell of wood smoke, and the firelight's warm glow flickered over the furniture.

Twelve-year-old Agatha had stroked the tip of her small, upturned nose, as she often did when she was thinking. "I'm still a newbie, Granddad," she'd said modestly. "For now, I enjoy digging up curious facts, describing interesting characters, and trying to work out good plot twists." She had opened the leather-bound notebook she carried with her at all times, showing her grandfather pages and pages of notes. "If it's all right with you, I'll pick your brain about hot-air ballooning tomorrow," she'd said. "You never know what research you might need for a character."

Granddad Ian had smoothed his thick white

beard and lit his pipe. He was a spry old man, wiry and strong, and liked to wear tweeds and a bow tie. Even though he'd been born in London, he'd been living in Scotland so long that he could easily pass for a wealthy local resident.

In his youth, Ian Mistery had made a fortune designing and building hot-air balloons for a famous company in Edinburgh, returning whenever he could to his peaceful country cottage in Bowden. In the world of hot-air ballooning, he was a star. His prototypes had been manufactured all over the world.

"Let's talk about your balloon trip. What do you and Dash want to do most before your parents arrive?" Granddad Ian had asked, puffing on his pipe.

Glancing over at her sleeping cousin, Agatha had reached into her purse for a map of the Highlands, the famous northern region of Scotland. Several destinations were circled in red

ink. "But no ruined castles this year," she'd said, passing the map to her granddad. "Dash thinks they're a total bore!"

"Would you rather go hunting for the Loch Ness monster?" Granddad Ian had asked her.

Agatha had rolled her eyes. "That's exactly what Dash wants to do," she'd said. "But I convinced him we should also visit the famous cairns and standing stones. I want to study ancient stone carvings for one of my stories."

"Excellent," Ian Mistery had agreed, putting on his bifocals to study their proposed route. He'd been about to speak when a giant shadow fell over the wall as a huge man lumbered into the room.

It was Chandler, Agatha's butler and jack-of-all-trades. Despite the former heavyweight boxer's imposing size, he had impeccable posture and wore a tailored tuxedo. "Please excuse my interruption," he had said quietly. "Miss Agatha,

I'm afraid there's a bit of a problem . . ."

"What is it?" the girl had asked.

"I was cleaning up the kitchen when I noticed that Watson has disappeared."

"No one's opened the doors," Granddad Ian had said, calmly blowing a smoke ring. "So wherever the rascal is hiding, he's still in the house."

"Let's take a look," Agatha had proposed.

They had split up to inspect the first floor of the house, calling the name of Agatha's white Siberian cat as they went through each room.

"Watson?" Agatha had whispered as she tiptoed down the dark hallways. "Where are you, kitty?"

After ten minutes of searching in vain, they'd met in the living room.

"Has anyone checked the pantry?" asked Chandler.

"Maybe he got scared and ran up to the

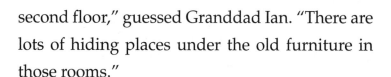

second floor," guessed Granddad Ian. "There are lots of hiding places under the old furniture in those rooms."

Agatha just shook her head. "Watson isn't a thief or a scaredy-cat," she had murmured. "If my memory serves me correctly, cats always look for a warm, sheltered nook when they arrive in a new place." She'd glanced around the room, then pushed her blond bangs from her forehead, listening intently. "Do you hear that noise?"

"What noise, Miss Agatha?" Chandler had asked.

"Do you mean Dash snoring?" Granddad Ian had laughed.

Agatha had moved toward her cousin and gently raised a corner of the plaid blanket that covered him from head to toe.

Nestled under the blanket, Watson was licking a paw and purring.

"Oh, kitty, what are you doing there?" Agatha

had whispered. "If Dash wakes up, he'll scare you to death with his screaming!"

Dash couldn't stand cats, especially Watson. In order to keep him from going ballistic, Agatha would need to move Watson without waking Dash.

She quietly had beckoned to Chandler. "Are you ready?" she'd asked him.

The butler had set his jaw.

They had moved in perfect unison. Chandler had lifted Dash in his brawny arms, and Agatha

had scooped up the cat just as he was about to unsheathe his claws. The butler then had carried the tall teenager into his bedroom as if he were a little boy, slipping him under the covers that Granddad Ian had pulled back silently. They all had tiptoed out of the room.

"Good job, Granddaughter," Ian had said when they were finished. "Very clever deduction!"

Agatha had smiled. "You have to train your powers of observation if you want to write mysteries," she said modestly.

Her granddad had stroked his beard, regarding her with admiration. There were rumors among their relatives that Agatha had extraordinary abilities for her age. She was a voracious reader with amazing intuition and a steel-trap memory for seemingly insignificant details. That evening, he'd also witnessed his granddaughter's talent for investigation.

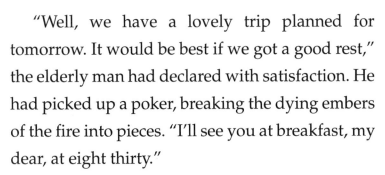

"Well, we have a lovely trip planned for tomorrow. It would be best if we got a good rest," the elderly man had declared with satisfaction. He had picked up a poker, breaking the dying embers of the fire into pieces. "I'll see you at breakfast, my dear, at eight thirty."

Agatha had nodded and gave him a tender hug. Moments later, he'd gone to his bedroom and fallen asleep. Agatha had curled up in her canopy bed, fluffed up a goose-feather pillow, and stuck her nose into a guidebook about Scotland that she'd brought from her parents' library in London.

When she woke the next morning, Agatha still had the open book in her hands.

She ran to the kitchen, where a mug of hot tea and fragrant blueberry scones were waiting for her.

There was no sign of Dash. Agatha rolled her eyes.

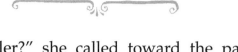

"Chandler?" she called toward the pantry. "Looks like somebody overslept for a change. Do you want to wake him this time or should I?"

A tap on the window surprised her. She turned to see Chandler outside, holding a gas tank for a hot-air balloon in his giant hands and sweating like a fountain. "If you're looking for Master Dash," he said, "he left a note saying he's gone into town for a meeting."

"A meeting?" she echoed. "Who is he meeting at eight in the morning?"

"I really couldn't say, Miss Agatha," Chandler said diplomatically.

Agatha was astonished. Her lazy cousin was up, dressed, and at a mysterious meeting? It was unbelievable! He'd just better get back home in time for their trip.

Agatha ate breakfast quickly, pulled on her clothes, and hurried out to the airfield with Watson trailing a few steps behind. The balloon

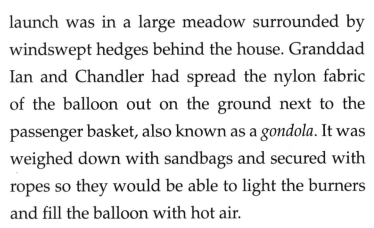

launch was in a large meadow surrounded by windswept hedges behind the house. Granddad Ian and Chandler had spread the nylon fabric of the balloon out on the ground next to the passenger basket, also known as a *gondola*. It was weighed down with sandbags and secured with ropes so they would be able to light the burners and fill the balloon with hot air.

Agatha's heart swelled with anticipation as she watched their preparations. The hot-air balloon was enormous, with panels divided into yellow segments.

"Did you see what I called my latest invention?" her grandfather called out in a welcoming tone, beckoning Agatha closer. He took her hand and led her onto the deflated balloon. The yellow fabric rippled under their feet, and when they got to the center, she noticed the writing in red block letters: *MISTERY BALLOON.*

"You made us a family balloon!" Agatha beamed. "Granddad, it's beautiful!"

"It will be even more beautiful up in the sky above the Highlands," said Ian Mistery with a smile, proudly hooking his thumbs under the suspenders he wore beneath his tweed jacket. "Everyone will wave at us as we pass by!"

Just then, Agatha spotted a bicycle shooting like a rocket down the path from the village. She knew it was Dash when he bumped over a rock and swerved into a tree, yelling "Ow!" so loudly that she knew he was fine.

Dash jumped off the broken bike and ran toward them, waving his arms.

"Hold everything!" he yelled. "Don't inflate that balloon!"

Calm as ever, Chandler asked, "What has happened, Master Dash?"

Dash was too winded to speak, but held up his EyeNet.

"His school must be sending him on a new mission," sighed Agatha. "I knew our trip to the Highlands was going to get sidetracked." A moment later, her smile returned as she asked, "So, Granddad, have you ever been part of an investigation?"

Voyage of the Mistery Balloon

The atmosphere at the airfield was suddenly charged with purpose. Still panting, Dash announced that their destination had changed. Instead of heading north toward the Highlands, they'd be traveling up the eastern coast of Scotland.

"We'd better take the Jeep, not the limo," he said, rubbing his injured elbow. "We have to get to a castle near Aberdeen, and the road's very winding."

"A castle? That's pretty ironic," joked Agatha. "Didn't you say they were boring?"

"Not anymore," said Dash. "Take a look." He

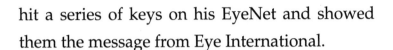

hit a series of keys on his EyeNet and showed them the message from Eye International.

AGENT DM14

PRECIOUS HISTORIC ARTIFACT STOLEN FROM DUNNOTTAR CASTLE, ABERDEEN, AT 8:35 A.M. GO THERE IMMEDIATELY AND SOLVE THE MYSTERY ASAP, OR YOU'LL GET A FAILING GRADE. DETAILS IN THE ATTACHED FILE.

Granddad Ian knew that Dash was enrolled in a detective school, but he had no idea the students' exams were real investigations. He was also beginning to sense that Agatha followed her cousin on his various missions around the world. These two children were Misteries through and through, always ready for an adventure!

Agatha was arguing with Dash about which car would be faster. Ian cleared his throat with a small cough to attract their attention. "With the

wind at our backs, the hot-air balloon will take us to Dunnottar Castle in no time," he said with a grin. Dash's and Agatha's jaws dropped as he added, "You're in a hurry, yes?"

Dash looked up at the cloudless sky. "How long will it take?" he asked doubtfully. "Will we get there by noon?"

A wry smile appeared above Granddad Ian's white beard. "Dear Grandson, I know a thousand shortcuts up there in the clouds," he said proudly. "Unless you'd rather share those winding back roads with tour buses, farmers, and stray herds of sheep. What do you think?"

There was a split second of indecision, broken by Agatha's gleeful voice. "I'm convinced, Granddad," she exclaimed. "Come on, Dash. Let's check out that file while they fill the balloon!"

Without missing a beat, their grandfather put his tweed jacket on the ground, rolled up his

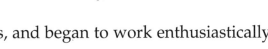

shirtsleeves, and began to work enthusiastically. "Let's get this balloon up as soon as we can!" he urged Chandler. "Fire up the gas jets!"

"As you wish, Mr. Mistery," the butler replied promptly.

As soon as they started to burn the propane gas, the balloon started to fill with warm air. It looked like a yellow cake rising inside an oven.

In the meantime, the two cousins ran to their grandfather's study to use his computer. The walls were covered with portraits and photographs of relatives who seemed to be looking over the cousins' shoulders.

"I feel like I'm being watched," said Dash, shifting uneasily.

He was always a little high-strung, but nothing made him more nervous than a detective-school exam.

To calm him down, Agatha took charge as usual. She searched through the file, printing

out everything she wanted to study while they were aloft. "This is a big pile of pages," she commented happily. "Now let's watch your pre-mission briefing!"

Dash looked as if he'd just woken up from a nightmare. "Oh yeah, right!" he exclaimed. He perched on Granddad's desk chair and studied the screen, with Agatha peering over his shoulder.

They both expected to see the mustached professor of Investigation Techniques, but instead, the screen filled with the image of an extremely thin woman with an ostrich-like neck, long eyelashes, and a fluffy mane of reddish hair.

The young detective swallowed in shock. *It was Agent MD38, the school principal! This must be really urgent!*

"Good morning, detective," the woman began. "As you already know, we've been contacted with an emergency. You are the closest agent to the scene, therefore your mission is of

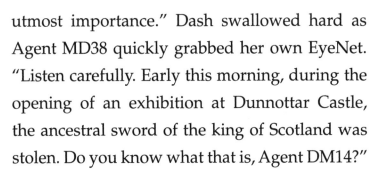

utmost importance." Dash swallowed hard as Agent MD38 quickly grabbed her own EyeNet. "Listen carefully. Early this morning, during the opening of an exhibition at Dunnottar Castle, the ancestral sword of the king of Scotland was stolen. Do you know what that is, Agent DM14?"

Dash turned to his cousin. "Please tell me you've got it stored in one of your famous memory drawers."

Agatha nodded yes, furiously scrawling notes in her notebook.

The principal's voice sounded urgent. "This case is especially puzzling," she said. "All the guests at the opening fell into a deep sleep at exactly the same time, and when they woke up, the sword had vanished. You'll find a full list of guests and staff in your file. Eye International was informed at once, before the police. They don't want the press to find out and start spreading rumors. No one has left the scene of the crime." She paused, looking serious. "Agent DM14, you must find the culprit and recover the sword by sundown. The agency's reputation is on the line. Make it work!"

The principal's face disappeared in a flash of purple light, as though she were a genie in a lamp.

"Your teachers are always so . . . colorful," Agatha said with a grin. Then she noticed that Dash looked frozen in terror.

"This case is too hard for a newbie like me!"

he sputtered. "I should never have turned on my EyeNet this morning. I'm such a jerk! I could still be hanging out with Dorothy instead of stuck in a wide world of trouble! I'm gonna be sick . . ."

"Don't panic, Dash!" Agatha interrupted. "We'll solve this mystery, you'll see!"

He blinked. "Do you really think so?"

"Of course," she assured him. "You can count on me. And Chandler and Granddad." She peered out the window, slipping the file pages into her purse. "Hey, look, the balloon is inflated!" Agatha grabbed her cousin by his wool sweater sleeve, dragging him out to the airfield.

The cousins climbed the steps into the gondola of the hot-air balloon and sat side by side on a tiny passenger bench. Chandler, who took up a full bench by himself, asked politely, "May we ascend now, Miss?"

Agatha nodded, excited. Dash gulped as Granddad Ian cast off the ropes, turned the flame

up high, and took the controls as the balloon slowly started to rise.

They had begun the most exciting part of the voyage. Everyone held their breath as they watched the landscape below, its green fields crisscrossed by stone fences. The cars on the lanes looked like miniature toys. Dash peered down at the village, wondering if Aileen had finished her haggis without him.

When the *Mistery Balloon* reached the right altitude to take advantage of the wind currents that would carry them northeast, Agatha turned to her cousin. "So, who is this Dorothy you'd rather be hanging out with than solving a case? If you don't mind my asking."

"Um, no one. Just a friend from when I was a kid," replied Dash, his face the color of a tomato.

His cousin winked at him. "Old friend, not new girlfriend?"

"What do you take me for?" Dash bristled.

"I'm a model detective!"

"Well then, model detective, you better keep your mind on the case," she teased him. "We need every inch of your precious brain!"

Chandler and Granddad Ian struggled to hold back their laughter.

As the balloon soared north past the capital city of Edinburgh, over the Firth of Forth, and into the Scottish countryside, the detectives pored over the files. Dash studied his EyeNet, and Agatha passed printout pages to Chandler as soon as she read them.

"You mentioned the king of Scotland's ancestral sword," said Granddad Ian. "Which king and what sword? I've lived here for decades, but there's so much history."

Agatha tapped the tip of her nose with her finger, concentrating. "It's a claymore belonging to Robert the Bruce, the warrior who freed the Scots from English rule in the Middle Ages. If my memory serves, he was king of Scotland from 1306 till—"

"What's a claymore?" Dash interrupted.

"A two-handed broadsword with a cross-shaped hilt and a short, powerful blade. It was the Scottish clans' traditional weapon. Like the ones you saw in *Braveheart*, though of course those were facsimiles . . ."

Without a word, Chandler handed Dash a photo.

"Thanks, Chandler," said Agatha. "A picture is worth a thousand words."

Their grandfather leaned over to study the photo. "Magnificent workmanship. Look at that hilt. Are those decorations bronze? There's no sign of oxidization," he noted. "How much is this heirloom worth?"

"Its value is mostly symbolic," replied Agatha. "According to the experts, it represents the unification of all the Scottish clans under one flag."

"So you don't think the thief wanted money?" Dash asked.

Agatha shook her head pensively. "It's too soon to tell," she sighed. She turned to Chandler. "Could I see that guest list again?" He handed it to her, and she quickly scanned the list of people attending the opening and their professional affiliations. "Looks like a lot of people who are passionate about antiques attended this event," she reflected. "So before we figure out a motive, we need to turn our attention to other details."

"Such as?" Dash prompted.

She paused for a moment, scratching Watson's ears as she contemplated the view below. The balloon was sailing above endless moors and small lakes, and the coastal town of Dundee could be seen in the distance. "What else do we have in the file?" she asked.

Chandler flipped through the pages, summarizing their contents in his usual few words: the history of the castle, short bios of the organizing committee and invited guests, and the transcript of the phone call made by the castle's director to Eye International. There was also a map of the castle grounds and some satellite images.

Dash nervously checked the time on his EyeNet.

"We'll study all these in detail and come up with a plan," proposed Agatha. "But first things first. What about something to eat?"

For the first time, Dash grinned. "Now you're talking!"

"I must confess, I'm a bit hungry myself," said Chandler.

Granddad Ian opened a picnic basket, passing out sandwiches. "Cheddar or marmalade?"

"Both!" said Dash happily.

Dunnottar Castle

$\mathcal{T}$he balloon floated over the rugged North Sea coast. Dash and Agatha gazed down at stone cliffs lashed by waves, sandy beaches, and harbor-seal colonies sunning on rocks. Granddad Ian kept his eye on the altimeter, adjusting their height to take advantage of more favorable winds. As promised, it was a speedy trip. "We'll be landing within half an hour," he announced with pride.

During the trip, all four passengers in the *Mistery Balloon* had pored over the files, exchanging opinions on what might have happened.

"Let's reconstruct the scene of the crime one last time," said Agatha. "The castle doors opened just after eight. By eight fifteen, everyone at the opening fell into a deep sleep, as if they had all inhaled chloroform. Everyone, that is, except for Ms. Ross, the personal assistant of the antiques dealer who organized the exhibition. She had exited the castle to look for the purse she'd left in her car. When she came back twenty minutes later, the king of Scotland's sword was gone and there were thirty people on the floor, fast asleep."

"When the guests came to, they reported strange dreams full of apparitions and sinister sounds," Dash continued. "To avoid a scandal in the press, the castle's director contacted Eye International instead of the police."

"And to assist with the investigation, he forbade anyone to leave the castle till sundown," Chandler concluded.

Dash frowned at the thought. "That would

be right," he sighed. "If we don't solve the case before dark, I can kiss my detective career good-bye!"

No one knew what to say to that. The balloon had begun its descent, and suddenly, they were surrounded by thick, misty clouds. It was like passing through a giant cotton ball that hid the castle from view.

This gave Granddad Ian an idea. "What if the sword is still inside the castle, but hidden away in some secret room?" he hypothesized. "Or maybe the thief hid it inside a crevice or cave in the cliffs?"

"That would be awesome!" Dash sounded hopeful. "Maybe we should focus on finding the sword, and figure out who stole it after we've gotten it back."

Agatha's eyes sparkled with mischief. "I just had a brainstorm!" she exclaimed, beaming.

Knowing her well, Dash asked bluntly, "What is it?"

Agatha stood up and started to pace in the limited space of the gondola, her head bowed and her index finger raised high. "I have a plan that might do the trick. It requires a bit of subterfuge."

Everybody stared at her, intrigued.

"What sort of subterfuge, Miss Agatha?" Chandler asked calmly.

She clasped her hands, rubbing her palms together. "What do you say we put on a performance?" she said. "Each of us will need to play a part."

Dash grinned. "Trust you to come up with something creative!"

But his smile didn't last long. Agatha explained their roles. Granddad Ian would play the part of the world-famous detective, Chandler would be his menacing bodyguard, and she and Dash would be bumbling apprentices.

"Why should I be an apprentice?" Dash groaned. "Especially a bumbling one?"

"Take a look at your outfit," said Agatha, casting her eyes up and down. "You look like a farmhand!"

While their Granddad laughed heartily, Dash covered his face in embarrassment. In their hurry to leave, he'd forgotten to change out of the scruffy clothes he'd picked for his meeting with Aileen.

"I don't understand," said Chandler. "Why are we playing these roles, Miss Agatha?"

"To create a diversion," she replied promptly. "While Granddad—the famous detective—interrogates all thirty guests, no one will pay any attention to me and Dash, searching the castle grounds for evidence—and the sword. You'll keep the guests in line. They'll be tired by now, and they'll be trying to leave the castle, but I'm sure you can figure out how to make them stay put . . . ," she said, giving Chandler a wink.

After a few more details, they were all

convinced that Agatha's strategy was ingenious. She drafted a list of questions for her grandfather to ask the witnesses, while Chandler studied the list of invited guests, and Dash pored over the map. They were concentrating so hard that they didn't realize they were right above Dunnottar Castle.

They heard shouted greetings below and leaned out over the edge to look down. A breathtaking sight met their eyes. The walled castle consisted of several buildings: a rugged stone tower, a stately manor house, and various ruins, all perched on the edge of a cliff overlooking the sea. There was only one entrance, a narrow road winding up from rolling hills to the steep, lonely headland. There were rows of cars parked in a field by the roadside.

Dunnottar Castle's reputation was well-deserved. It really did seem impregnable.

Granddad Ian pulled out his pocket watch.

"Noon on the dot." He beamed. "We made perfect time, just as I promised!"

The children congratulated him as he prepared to land.

A group of people clustered in the grassy square in the center of the castle grounds. Agatha noticed that they all wore elegant clothes befitting an exhibition opening; some of the men even wore traditional kilts. The only detail that surprised her was the police car parked on the side of the road, just outside the castle walls.

She immediately pointed it out to Chandler. "Didn't the file say they weren't going to notify the police of the theft?"

"I don't think they have, Miss Agatha," he replied. "It's a standard security detail. I suspect those two policemen out there know nothing about the missing sword."

"Right," she said sharply. "And we certainly won't be the ones to inform them."

When the hot-air balloon landed inside the square, maneuvered precisely to the last millimeter, the guests broke out in applause. Then a short, anxious bald man with glasses sent everyone back inside the manor house, leaving only the organizing committee to greet the new arrivals.

"Welcome, Agent DM14," said the bald man.

Agatha gently elbowed her Granddad, who was busily shutting off gas valves.

He turned around, waving his hat in greeting. "Thank you. And you must be Mr. MacKenzie, the castle director," he replied, squinting shrewdly.

"Aye," said the bald man. "May I introduce these fine gentlemen?"

"I'd be delighted!" Granddad Ian replied with a knowing smile.

Agatha watched closely as her grandfather shook the hands of Professor Cunningham, the antiques dealer who organized the exhibition, and his two main investors. The haughty, red-mustached Earl of Duncan barely extended his hand, and portly oil millionaire Angus Snodgrass looked annoyed and impatient.

They were all impressed by Chandler's hulking stature, and barely noticed the two young apprentices. Everything was going according to plan.

"Well," Director MacKenzie said, "there's no time to waste. Let me take you to the arms hall so you can begin your investigation."

The committee escorted them inside the castle manor, where the odor of fresh paint still hung in the air from the recent restorations. They passed through the arched entry hall and entered a high-ceilinged room full of weapons, shields, and suits of armor. There was an empty fireplace big enough to roast a whole ox, surrounded by displays of medieval artifacts and mannequins wearing traditional Scottish kilts.

The guests stood in small clusters throughout the room, looking tired, unhappy, and restless. A few of them nibbled on tea sandwiches and reception hors d'oeuvres. They were probably fed up with waiting so long.

It was a well-heeled crowd, including some noblemen wearing their family tartans, a few well-known artists and athletes, business people, and local politicians. There was a little girl with her aunt, a professional photographer, and a bored-looking bagpiper wearing a full-dress kilt with a tasseled sporran. Agatha noticed a young woman seated off to one side, looking distressed, and guessed this must be the professor's assistant, Ms. Ross.

Director MacKenzie led them to the center of the hall and stopped in front of an empty glass case.

"This is where the king of Scotland's sword was displayed," explained Professor Cunningham.

Tall and charming, with designer frames for his glasses, he looked to be in his late thirties. "As you can see, the thief got into the cabinet without breaking the glass," he observed. "I advised the use of security cameras . . . but nobody listened to me!"

"You weren't footing the bill for them, were you, Professor?" The Earl of Duncan turned red with agitation. "I bet you've never had to fork out a penny in your entire life!"

"All you do is blather and gripe," Snodgrass snapped, raising the temperature of the argument even higher.

"Calm down, calm down!" Director MacKenzie urged, sounding anxious. "We cannot continue to blame one another!"

Granddad Ian gave a little cough, but the committee members didn't stop bickering until Chandler loomed over them, cracking his knuckles and fixing them with a grim stare.

"Let's stay out of this," Agatha whispered in her cousin's ear. "We should get out of here ASAP and leave the questions to Granddad."

"You think he'll be able to get any useful information?" Dash whispered back. "The only thing these guys seem good at is arguing!"

"Don't worry, they're all scared of Chandler." Agatha smiled. "He's pretty good at keeping people in line."

She nodded to Granddad Ian. He stood in the center of the room, explaining how he intended to conduct the interrogations. A few guests protested, but he warned them all that complaints should be directed to his bodyguard.

Chandler confirmed this with an intimidating grunt, and the room fell silent.

In an authoritative tone, Granddad Ian announced that nobody would leave the room, except his apprentices. He thanked the guests for their patience, and headed into Director

MacKenzie's private office, where he planned to interview the suspects in order, one by one.

The Mistery cousins could start on their mission at last!

Trouble in the Tower

"Your plan's working perfectly," Dash gloated as they left the manor house. "Nobody will bother us for a while now."

Agatha was already scanning the nearby ruins with her investigator's gaze. "Pass me the castle plans?" she asked.

"Uh sure, here they are!"

"And the satellite photos?"

Dash pulled up a scan on his EyeNet and zoomed in on the image. "Let's start with this crumbling building and then hit the tower," he proposed.

"I agree," replied Agatha. "Keep your eyes

open for clues." she added as they entered a ruined chapel near the castle walls. Only a perimeter of loose stones remained between tufts of high grass.

"Notice anything?" asked Dash, poking the soil.

"The grass over here has been trampled," replied Agatha. "But the tracks don't look recent. I'm thinking the painters came through this way on their way to the arms hall. Look, here's a scrape from a ladder they dragged in the mud."

"What's significant about that?"

Agatha shrugged. "The thief wasn't the first person to walk on this grass. So we might find a lot of red herrings."

"Red herrings?"

Agatha rolled her eyes. Didn't her cousin know anything? "It's mystery-writer slang for false leads."

CHAPTER FOUR

Dash held up a small object. "You mean like this weird bamboo straw?"

Agatha looked at it closely, stroking the tip of her nose. "Well done, Dash!" she exclaimed, wide-eyed. "You've uncovered our first real clue!"

He shook his head, stunned. "A clue? But it's only a straw!"

"Look closely." Agatha covered the end with a handkerchief and blew into it, creating a deep whistling sound. "I should open my memory drawers more often," she said, satisfied. "This little tube is a drone reed for bagpipes; I'm sure of it!"

Dash scratched his chin. "There's a piper inside, Griffin Mulligan. Are you suggesting he might have dropped it here?" he asked. "What would that prove?"

"We can question him when we get back," said Agatha, slipping the reed into a ziplock bag.

She never left behind anything that might be useful later. "Come on, let's use that intuition of yours to uncover more clues."

But it wasn't Dash who found the next one.

They were working their way along the wall toward an old stone well when they noticed Watson scampering around the lawn, batting something between his front paws.

"Can't you put that beast on a leash?" muttered Dash. "He does nothing but eat, sleep, and play!"

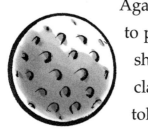

Agatha glared at him and knelt down to pet her cat. It was only then that she noticed the golf ball between his claws. "Check the guest list," she told Dash. "There's a professional golfer on it, if I'm not mistaken."

"You're right," he replied, running his finger down the page. "Jim 'Cheetah' Karp, an international champion!"

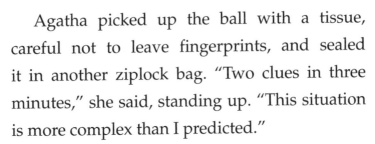

Agatha picked up the ball with a tissue, careful not to leave fingerprints, and sealed it in another ziplock bag. "Two clues in three minutes," she said, standing up. "This situation is more complex than I predicted."

"Why is it more complex?"

"The more clues we find," she replied drily, "the more suspects we have, and the more confused our ideas will get."

"What about this peacock feather?" Dash grabbed it off a thistle, where it was fluttering in the breeze. "I think there was a lady with a feathered hat inside . . ."

"There certainly was," grumbled

Agatha, sticking the feather into yet another plastic bag. "But how did it get here?"

"Maybe it blew off her hat when we arrived in the hot-air balloon."

"That lady is very heavy and walks with a cane. I don't remember her coming outside to greet us." Agatha strode toward the well, thinking hard. It was a large, octagonal basin, about sixteen feet deep and full of dark, slimy water with green algae floating on top. "This would be the perfect place to hide the sword," she reflected.

Dash leaned over to look, then pulled his head back fast. "It stinks like a sewer," he groaned. "You don't want us to scour the bottom, do you?"

"Got your swimsuit?" joked Agatha. Then she turned serious. "To really check what's down there, the well would need to be drained." She tapped her nose and peered into the depths with her flashlight. "I think I can see something shiny," she whispered, intrigued.

But the gleam she'd spotted must have just been a reflection, because it did not reappear as she swept the light back and forth.

Dash got impatient. "I don't see a thing. Let's move on to the tower," he said. "I don't know how long Granddad will be able to keep questioning witnesses."

Agatha glanced at his EyeNet. "You're right, it's nearly two," she agreed.

They zigzagged quickly between the ruined buildings until they reached the edge of the cliff, where a massive stone tower loomed.

Its top floor was crumbling and riddled with holes from battering rams and cannonballs, but it still maintained its aura of grandeur.

The two cousins went through the heavy door, moving silently as though the ancient stone walls might still be concealing an enemy.

"We're right in the heart of Dunnottar Castle," whispered Agatha as they entered a circular

chamber. "Do you know when the first stone was laid?"

Dash shook his head, clueless.

"Experts have dated it to the fifth century," explained Agatha, sounding as if she were quoting one of the history books she was always reading. "It was built by the Picts as a fortress. Then it was invaded by the Vikings, and ever since then it's been occupied by Scottish clans and English conquerors."

"Cool," murmured Dash, shivering as they crossed into another dank room. Then he added, "Could I see that flashlight? It's pitch-black in here!"

Agatha turned on her flashlight and lit up their path. Not a moment too soon, because Dash was about to step into a hole!

He jumped back with a cry of surprise and tripped over a pickax, sprawling across the stone floor.

"Don't touch anything!" shouted Agatha. "There may be precious clues!"

Dash got up, brushing fresh dirt from his clothes. "Clues?" he hissed. "I almost fell into a hole!" Then his expression changed. "But why is there a hole here?"

"Exactly," said Agatha, shining her flashlight beam inside. "The thief could have dug this hole to get rid of the sword."

Dash joined her as they were hit with a gust of cold air from below. "Let's check out the plans," he said.

They unfolded the map and immediately spotted a secret passageway under the floor. "This goes all the way down through the cliff and winds up on the beach," said Agatha.

"And our thief knew it!"

"He must have broken through the floor at the weakest point," continued the girl, casting an eye at the pickax. "But something's not right."

"What?" asked Dash.

Agatha moved the flashlight beam in a circle. "The hole is too narrow for a person to pass through," she noted. "Unless the thief passed the stolen goods down to an accomplice below . . ."

"Who could have escaped from the beach in a motorboat!" Dash finished.

Just then, Watson appeared out of nowhere and jumped into the hole. "No, kitty! What are you doing?" cried Agatha in desperation.

"That cat is insane!" yelled her cousin.

Agatha called Watson's name over and over. After a while they heard his meows echoing up from under the floor. Agatha began to pace back and forth, with no idea what to do next. Finally she stopped, grabbing hold of the pickax. "We have to go after him!" she declared.

"But you said not to touch anything!"

"Well, I've changed my mind!"

With powerful strikes of the pickax, Agatha

knocked a few stones loose so that she and Dash could fit through. She explored the passage with her flashlight. "Luckily it looks like it's still in good shape," she said. "But the ceiling is very low." She lowered herself down, shining the flashlight in front of her, then signaled to Dash to follow.

As they crept down the long tunnel, she kept calling for Watson, and he answered with plaintive meows.

It took half an hour to reach the beach at the foot of the cliff. When Dash and Agatha finally emerged, they blinked in the bright sunlight.

Watson was chasing a fiddler crab and looked at them, surprised. "Bad kitty!" Agatha reprimanded him, cuddling him tight in her arms. "You scared me to death!"

Despite himself, Dash breathed a sigh of relief, too. Then he tapped Agatha's shoulder. "Look at the sand."

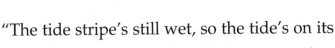

"The tide stripe's still wet, so the tide's on its way out," observed Agatha. "If the accomplice fled in a boat . . ."

"The high tide has erased his footprints for good," finished Dash.

They looked at each other. Agatha held up her cat, and they made their way back to the castle, discouraged.

Granddad Ian, Master Detective

gatha and Dash arrived back at the manor just after 3:00 and went straight to the director's office. They nodded to Chandler, who stood at his post by the door like a guard outside Buckingham Palace, and went inside.

As Dash laid the pickax and the other clues on the floor, Agatha noticed their grandfather's dazed expression.

"Are you all right?" she asked.

"These people are out of their minds!" Ian Mistery said, his voice shaking a bit. "I interviewed thirty people, and every single one of them told me something different. The details

all contradict one another, and everyone blames someone else!"

The unflappable hot-air balloonist was visibly shaken.

"First things first," Agatha said as she sat down beside him. "Did you take notes on the witness statements as I suggested?"

"Of course," he replied, pushing a notebook across the desk. "One page for each guest, with detailed accounts of everything they saw and heard before they fell asleep, and their crackpot theories about what happened."

"Did you find any common themes?" Dash intervened eagerly. "Do the witnesses agree on any key points?"

"Do you want the truth?" their grandfather asked enigmatically. "Are you sure?"

A little thrown by the question, Dash shrugged and said, "Um, it would be a good starting point . . ."

"The answer is no!" Granddad Ian practically shouted. "Not in the least! It's just random nonsense!"

Agatha decided she'd better step in. She thanked Granddad Ian, gave him a reassuring hug, and skimmed through his notebook of statements. The handwriting was old-fashioned, tiny, and full of flourishes. The information was recorded in proper order, with the precision of an accountant. "You've done an excellent job," she said gratefully. "Now, let's line up the statements and weed out the ones that are useless."

"That's how we detectives work," confirmed Dash, suddenly hopeful again. "We narrow the field so we can focus on the most likely suspects."

Agatha flashed him a knowing smile and made room for him at the table. "Who should we start with, dear Granddad?"

Feeling comforted, Granddad Ian flipped through the notebook and pointed to a page.

"This madman insists that he heard a gunshot. I had Chandler frisk all the guests, but he didn't find any firearms."

"Why bother?" Dash said. "The witnesses were all out cold, so the thief wouldn't have to resort to violence."

Granddad Ian turned the page. "This woman, a publicist with a nervous twitch, claims she saw a ghost walking upside down on the ceiling," he said. "What do you think? Is she—?"

"Next!" Agatha cut him off.

"All right, how about the still-life painter who heard a wolf howl in the hall?" Granddad Ian continued, undaunted.

"I'd say he's got some kind of imagination!" Dash snickered.

Agatha chewed on her lip, deep in thought. "Are we sure it's just imagination?" she asked.

"You don't really think Castle Dunnottar has ghosts and wolves, do you?" Dash wondered.

"Of course not," said Agatha. "But I'm wondering what substance might cause such hallucinations."

"Maybe they were nightmares caused by the sudden sleepiness?" Ian Mistery wondered. "It can happen."

"Exactly," said Agatha, tapping her nose. "But why were they suddenly sleepy? We need to find out how everyone fell asleep at the same time."

"So we're not going to keep reading

statements?" asked Dash. "Too bad. I was really enjoying them!"

"Agatha's right," said Ian Mistery. "The main issue is what kind of substance was used to put all the guests to sleep instantly. Any ideas?"

"Chloroform needs to be inhaled at close range," reflected his granddaughter. "But there are other sleep-inducing substances that can be injected or swallowed. What do you think, Dash?"

"I'd rule out injections," replied her cousin. "Too hard to administer."

"I agree. And the guests hadn't had anything to eat or drink yet when they fell asleep. The catered reception was scheduled for noon," observed Agatha.

"So it must have been some sort of gas," concluded Dash. "But how was it distributed?"

"If my memory serves me correctly, Ms. Ross found the windows wide open, right,

Granddad?" asked Agatha.

He nodded. "That's what she said when I questioned her," he confirmed. "If the room was pumped full of gas, it was fully dispersed by the time she got back."

Dash slammed his palm on the table. "What if she did it?" he said excitedly. "Maybe she released the gas into the arms hall and used her purse as an excuse to go outside while it took effect. Then she came back with a handkerchief over her nose, stole the sword, passed it to her accomplice, and opened the windows to wake everyone up!" He punctuated his flood of words by putting both feet on the table with a satisfied clunk. "Case closed, folks!"

Agatha wasn't convinced, but she decided to indulge him. "Even if your assumptions are correct, we need to find proof. Not to mention the sword."

"Would you like to question Ms. Ross again?"

asked their granddad, heading for the door.

Just as he was about to open it, Agatha stopped him. "To catch your prey, you need to bait the trap," she said, smiling shrewdly.

The others stared blankly as she summarized all the clues they had found so far, emphasizing that if Ms. Ross was the culprit, she would have needed help from an accomplice, who presumably carried the sword through the secret passage, escaping by sea. Then she went to the door and whispered to Chandler to gather the organizing committee together.

"As you wish, Miss Agatha," the butler replied politely. Then he remembered that he was supposed to act like a tough guy, and growled, "I'll bring 'em right in, little girl!"

The organizing committee came into the office moments later, eager to hear if there was any news. Ian Mistery sat with the depositions in front of him as though he had everything under

control, and his "apprentices" sat in the corner.

"In my line of work, we don't use the word 'news' until the investigation is completed," Ian Mistery said. "I've asked you back to explain a few things."

"What things?" Director MacKenzie sounded alarmed. His bald head glistened with sweat. "I hope we're not suspects in this theft?"

The Earl of Duncan traded frowns with his colleague Snodgrass, the North Sea oil millionaire. "Maybe you should put Professor Cunningham in handcuffs for his incompetence," he sneered. "We'd all be delighted!"

Behind him, Chandler loudly cracked his knuckles. A tense silence fell over the room.

"None of you is a suspect," Ian Mistery reassured them. "But you need to tell me whatever you can about young Ms. Ross."

All eyes turned toward Professor Cunningham. "Ms. Ross?" he repeated, sounding surprised. "I can't tell you much, to be honest. I hired her as an assistant last month, to help set up this exhibition. She's very smart but doesn't work well under pressure. She tends to forget things."

Dash interrupted. "Are you referring to the misplaced purse, Professor?"

If the antiques dealer was startled to hear from a teenage apprentice, he didn't let on. "Not just that," he replied. "Ms. Ross simply isn't reliable. She can't even make decent coffee." He paused, then added indifferently, "I'm planning to fire her tomorrow."

Until he mentioned coffee, Agatha had felt sympathy for the handsome professor, but his coldness annoyed her. "What was so important in that purse?" she asked, struggling to maintain her calm.

Professor Cunningham smoothed back his hair. "Official documents from the Museum of Edinburgh," he said with a bitter sigh. "Without them, we don't have permission to exhibit the king of Scotland's sword here at Dunnottar Castle. And we're going to owe the museum a huge sum of money!"

The Case of the Missing Purse

As soon as they heard the words *huge sum of money*, the committee members exploded with fury. Chandler needed all of his skills as a bouncer to calm them down.

Snodgrass, the oil tycoon, was the most agitated, threatening to strangle Professor Cunningham with his bare hands. "You'll pay dearly for this, you academic runt!" he shouted. "I paid good money to set up this exhibition, and you've ruined everything. I'm going to sue your fancy pants off!"

Chandler intervened, steering him into a chair.

The Case of the Missing Purse

The other committee members showed their distress in various ways. Director MacKenzie muttered over and over that his reputation was ruined, and the Earl of Duncan sneered at the professor, who sat with his head in his hands, as if his whole career in antiquities had just gone up in flames.

"Gentlemen, listen!" cried Granddad Ian. "Try to compose yourselves! This chaos is hindering my investigation!"

"How can you still have any doubts, detective?" Snodgrass asked haughtily. "Arrest Ms. Ross and end this farce one and for all!"

Dash shot Agatha a glance that said: *"What did I tell you?"*

She didn't react, but whispered something to her granddad.

Ian Mistery nodded. "I'll ask you gents to step out of my office," he ordered in a tone that invited no arguments. "I will cross-examine Ms.

Ross and let you know the outcome."

The organizing committee seemed relieved, and Chandler escorted them out of the office, still quarreling among themselves.

While the butler went to call Ms. Ross for a final interview, Agatha peeked into the arms hall and saw the guests stirring restlessly, wondering what had just happened.

She closed the door, staring into space for a moment.

The hands of the clock clicked onward inexorably. It was already 4:30.

Agatha whispered her new plan into her granddad's ear, then returned to her spot in the corner. Relaxing in his armchair, Dash shook his head. "You're so stubborn, cousin," he goaded her. "You don't give in even when all of the evidence points the same way!"

"Does it?" asked Agatha. "If you ask me, Ms. Ross is innocent."

Before Dash could respond, they heard a soft knock at the door. They answered in chorus, "Come in!"

A pretty girl in her twenties entered. She wore a tailored suit and makeup that seemed like an effort to make herself look older and more professional. She looked scared and dejected as she took a seat in front of the desk, with her hands in her lap and her head bowed. "How can I help you, detective?" she whispered without raising her gaze.

Their granddad adjusted his bow tie; it was the signal he and Agatha had agreed on. Agatha took a seat next to the young assistant, trying to catch her evasive eyes.

"Who is your accomplice, Ms. Ross?" she asked point-blank. "And what kind of boat did he use?"

Ms. Ross's head jolted up and she looked around, frightened. "My accomplice?" she stammered. "What boat? What do you mean?" She seemed genuinely confused.

Even Dash paid attention. Granddad Ian nodded at him to stay quiet and passed the notebook of witness statements to Agatha.

"Your statement is recorded here," the girl continued in a gentler tone. "You're the only person who wasn't inside the arms hall, which makes you the chief suspect in the theft. You understand, don't you?"

Ms. Ross nodded, not saying a word.

Agatha was used to evaluating people's facial expressions on the spot, and she was convinced the assistant was innocent. But she needed to keep pumping her for as much information as

possible. "So you didn't widen the hole with a pickax and pass the sword to an accomplice?" she asked Ms. Ross.

"I'm sorry, but I have no idea what you're talking about," she replied.

"Tell us exactly what you did this morning," pressed Agatha, wanting to delve deeper. "Give us every detail of what happened from the moment you drove up to Dunnottar Castle this morning."

The trembling assistant took a deep breath and began to talk. She had arrived at 7:15 and found Professor Cunningham in the director's office. The organizing committee was double-checking that everything was in place in the arms hall before the exhibition opened at 8:00. The professor had asked her to bring him some coffee from the machine in the kitchen at the rear of the manor. It had taken her a while, because she'd never used that kind of coffee machine

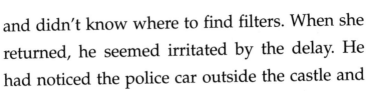

and didn't know where to find filters. When she returned, he seemed irritated by the delay. He had noticed the police car outside the castle and asked her for the exhibition permits.

Ms. Ross paused for a moment to catch her breath. "The professor was so nervous," she continued. "He kept looking outside, where the guests were already lining up outside the door. I had put the permits in my purse, but I couldn't find it anywhere. When I told Mr. Cunningham, he was furious!"

"What did you do?" asked Granddad Ian.

"I looked all over the office, but I couldn't find it," explained Ms. Ross. "Meanwhile, Director MacKenzie and the others had gone to the entrance to let the guests in. Professor Cunningham ordered me to go out to my car, since it was the only place I could have left my purse, and to come back with the permits. So I slipped out the side door as the guests started to enter."

"Did anybody notice you leave?" Agatha interrupted.

"I don't think so." She wavered.

Agatha pushed her hair out of her eyes and gave her a clever smile. "Not even the two policemen in the parking lot?"

The young woman didn't even need to think about it.

"Oh. They definitely noticed me," she replied, blushing a little. "While I was searching the trunk, looking for my purse, they came over and asked me if I was a soccer fan, and who I was rooting for in the World Cup."

"Why would they ask you something so stupid?" Dash asked, surprised.

Agatha and Granddad Ian looked at him. "Tell me you always say intelligent things when you're trying to flirt with a girl?" his cousin said with a laugh. "Like, what did you ask Dorothy when you met her for breakfast this morning?"

Dash flushed beet red and fell silent.

Granddad Ian picked up where Agatha had left off. "Your purse wasn't in the car, am I right?" he asked the witness.

"I looked everywhere, even under the seats, but it wasn't there," replied Ms. Ross. "So I went back to the castle, sure that Professor Cunningham was going to be furious, but he was lying on the ground with everybody else."

Agatha checked the notebook. "It was eight thirty-five a.m. You were outside for twenty minutes," she read calmly. "When you returned, you saw that the sword had been stolen, and you woke up Director MacKenzie. The rest of the story we know."

Ms. Ross nervously twisted her hair. She looked as if she was going to cry as she added, "You have to believe me. I'm positive I had my purse with me when I came into the castle this morning. I was in a hurry, and I was carrying a

lot of papers, so maybe I dropped it, but I don't know where!"

"Or maybe someone made it disappear," suggested Agatha. Before Dash could protest, she thanked the witness and asked one last question. "Can you describe your purse for me, Ms. Ross?"

"It's a shoulder bag, light brown leather, with a brass buckle." This said, she thanked them politely and scurried out of the office.

Agatha looked at her granddad and said, "Girls can forget many things, but never their purses!"

"That doesn't prove she's innocent," Dash cried, jumping to his feet. "She might have made up that whole story!"

"Do you really believe that?"

"Yes, I believe that!" he fumed. "Nothing she said can be proven!"

Agatha glanced at the clock. "That's where you're wrong, cousin," she said. "Let's take a little walk."

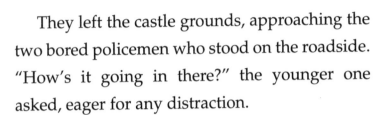

They left the castle grounds, approaching the two bored policemen who stood on the roadside. "How's it going in there?" the younger one asked, eager for any distraction.

"The opening ceremony was wonderful," Agatha lied through her teeth. Then she asked if they'd met a young woman looking for her

purse that morning. The two policemen looked at each other, muttering something vague, but Agatha didn't give up. "You asked her if she was a soccer fan, if that rings any bells. Talked about the World Cup?" The policemen adjusted their hats and confirmed the times that Ms. Ross had reported.

Even though it was clear that the assistant was telling the truth, Dash didn't give up. "What about this missing purse of hers? Who took it, and where is it now?"

"All in good time, Dash," said Agatha. "All in good time!"

Clueless

*T*he sun was sinking low, and sinister shadows stretched over the courtyard of Dunnottar Castle. Agatha calculated that they had barely an hour left to solve the mystery.

"So where are we going?" asked Dash, alarmed by this news. "Shouldn't we try to track down the accomplice who's got the sword?"

"There is no accomplice, dear cousin," Agatha said as they entered the gardener's shed.

"Are you crazy?" said Dash. "Then why is there a new hole in the floor of the tower? What about the secret passage that leads down to the

beach? Where else would the sword be, and how was it stolen?"

"I don't know yet," said Agatha. "But I think we're on the right track." She found a garden rake and got Dash to lash a long bamboo pole to the handle with duct tape. He kept complaining about wasting time, but he knew enough to trust Agatha's hunches.

They walked back to the well with the extra-long pole.

"Lower it and scour the bottom," said Agatha. "I bet there's a surprise inside this stinking well!"

The first thing Dash brought up was a mass of decayed blackish leaves, but on the next pass, he hooked something heavy. As he started to pull it up, Agatha spotted a glint of brass.

"That's what I saw shining!" she said, glowing. "It's Ms. Ross's purse!"

Stunned, Dash redoubled his efforts and pulled up the purse. It was soaking and stained,

but when Agatha carefully opened the brass clasp, she discovered the permits were safe inside a plastic bag.

"Do you still think she's guilty?" she asked.

"No way," replied Dash, congratulating himself on his logic. "If she were the thief, she wouldn't have thrown her own purse in a well— or wasted time going to look for it."

They left the rake on the grass, and hurried inside to show Granddad Ian and Chandler their find.

"That narrows the number of suspects to four," said Chandler.

"Why?" Dash asked, puzzled.

"The culprit must be on the organizing committee," Chandler said, calm as ever. "The purse was dropped into the well before the castle was open to the public."

Agatha snapped her fingers. "Your reasoning is flawless, Chandler," she said. "And I think I

know why our thief tried to make the permits disappear!"

The others fell silent, hanging on her words.

"Ms. Ross said she found everybody asleep," explained the girl. "But we know that the thief was awake, and had twenty minutes to commit the crime while she was searching for them!"

"I knew I didn't care for those fellows," declared Ian Mistery. "But how do we figure out which one is the thief? I don't know who's the least trustworthy, Director MacKenzie, the Earl of Duncan, or that arrogant rich guy, Snodgrass!"

Dash cut in. "Hold on a minute. Agatha and I found some clues in the ruins, near the well where the thief hid the purse." He pointed at the pickax and ziplock bags in the corner. "If we add up all the clues and Granddad's witness statements, what do we get?"

"They're all just red herrings," said Agatha. "The thief scattered a bunch of false clues to

create havoc in the crime scene."

"What about the bagpipe reed?" Dash asked stubbornly. "'I still think we should question the piper."

"The thief must have taken it from his instrument while he was sleeping," said Agatha. "Maybe he doesn't like Scottish music!"

Everyone laughed, except Dash. "And how about the golf ball?" he said. "Shouldn't we read the file on that professional golfer, Panther or whatever?"

"Cheetah Karp," replied Agatha, "is a famous collector of medieval weapons. The thief figured we'd find that out in our research and wanted to send us down a blind alley with that as a possible motive. Nice try, but it didn't work."

"And the peacock feather? Is that lady a suspect?"

"I suspect she has bad taste in hats," replied Agatha. "But that's about all."

Dash didn't even bother to ask about the hole and the pickax, since Agatha had already assured him there was no accomplice. So all of their clues were useless.

Chandler excused himself to stand guard in the arms hall. He took his role in their act very seriously. Granddad Ian turned to his granddaughter with the notebook of statements. "Don't you think it might be wise to reread these, now that we've narrowed the field? We might find something important."

"Great idea," said Agatha.

Even Dash agreed.

They flipped through the pages, commenting aloud whenever something came to mind.

"Remember the publicist who said she saw an upside-down ghost?" said Dash. "I bet it was the thief's shadow when he took the sword out of the cabinet."

"And the wolf howl was probably the wind

blowing in though the windows he opened," said Agatha.

"What about the gunshot?" asked Granddad Ian. "How can we explain that?"

"Maybe he just broke something?" Dash suggested. "What do you think, Agatha?"

She was silent, rereading a page.

"Agatha?" Dash repeated.

"The photographer!" she exclaimed suddenly. "Granddad, what did he tell you?"

Ian Mistery slowly loosened his bow tie. "He was distraught that his digital camera was broken," he said. "It slipped out of his hand when he fell asleep on the floor, so he wasn't able to finish his job."

"I doubt that's exactly what happened," said Agatha. "It could have been dropped on purpose by our clever thief, and maybe it took some incriminating shots!"

"I'll go get it and see if the memory card's still

intact," offered Dash.

"Go as fast as you can, Superman!" said Agatha.

He disappeared instantly.

Agatha glanced at the clock on the wall. It was 5:15. How long did they have until sundown? The sky was already beginning to show the first tinges of evening color.

Luckily Dash was as quick as his name. "I'm sure I can recover the images!" he shouted enthusiastically. "I'll scan the memory card with my EyeNet, and we'll be able to see the photos in just a few minutes!"

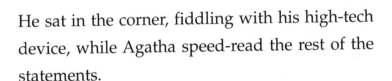

He sat in the corner, fiddling with his high-tech device, while Agatha speed-read the rest of the statements.

Granddad Ian watched proudly as his grandchildren worked. "I don't want to disturb you," he said, "but we still don't know how the guests were put to sleep. Are you sure it was an anesthetic gas?"

Agatha put down the notebook, thinking it over. "If we figure out how the substance was distributed, it might lead us right to the culprit," she mused. "And we know this thief has done his best to mislead us at every turn."

"So where does that leave us?"

"If we consider it carefully, why did he open the windows in the hall?" asked Agatha. "Maybe that's another red herring!"

"That puts us right back where we started."

She rubbed her nose furiously. "Not at all," she said. "I just opened one of my memory

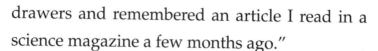

drawers and remembered an article I read in a science magazine a few months ago."

"What did it say?" Ian Mistery asked.

"A group of Japanese scientists was doing experimental research on anesthetics," said Agatha as if in a trance. Suddenly her eyes lit up. "That's it, I've got it!" she exclaimed. "These doctors discovered a kind of powder derived from chloroform that acts on contact with the skin. The side effects include strong hallucinations and it only lasts a short time."

"How short?" asked her granddad. "Twenty minutes?"

"If memory serves, between fifteen and twenty minutes."

"That's it!" Granddad

exclaimed. "The thief must have used this chloroform powder!"

Agatha shook her head. "But where did he put it? Is there something everyone touched, except for Ms. Ross?"

The question hung in the air as Dash jumped up, holding his EyeNet. "I downloaded the photos!" he yelled in excitement. "Let's take a look!"

Agatha and Granddad Ian stared at him in silence.

"What did I miss?" asked Dash Mistery.

CHAPTER EIGHT

The King of Scotland's Sword

As soon as the sun went below the horizon, Dunnottar Castle's weary guests rose from their tables, eager to leave. They found Agatha and Dash standing in front of the castle gate with Granddad Ian, Chandler, and the two policemen who had spent the day outside the castle walls.

"Don't you want to know who stole the king of Scotland's sword?" said Agatha with a wide grin.

The guests shifted anxiously. "You're not planning to keep us all night, are you?" snapped golf champion Cheetah Karp.

"If we've waited patiently until sunset, it's

only to avoid the indignity of dealing with policemen and journalists," sniffed the lady with the feathered hat. "So what are these officers doing here?"

"I'm hungry!" shrieked the little girl.

"The police are here to arrest the person who stole the sword," Dash explained. "Then you'll be free to go back to your homes and forget all about this long day!"

Minutes later, they sat in rows in the arms hall, as if they were the audience for a play. The performers were four English detectives and a Siberian cat who'd arrived in a hot-air balloon.

Behind them, a projector screen was set up to show slides.

The organizing committee was even more agitated than their guests.

"What is the meaning of this?" huffed an enraged Earl of Duncan, as Angus Snodgrass folded his arms, glaring.

"Why are we all being held here?" demanded Professor Cunningham. "Was this your idea, director?"

MacKenzie anxiously rubbed his hand over his shiny bald head, indicating that he was as much in the dark as they were.

"Ladies and gentlemen, please, take your seats. There are a few chairs in the front row," Ian Mistery invited. "Now, I would like your complete attention!"

At these words, everybody fell silent.

"Good. Now the show can begin," he announced, sounding like a TV host. "I'll hand everything over to my assistant, the brilliant detective, Agatha Mistery!"

All eyes were on Agatha. At first, she was a little intimidated, but as soon as she started to reconstruct their investigation, she regained her natural confidence.

Her narration was accompanied by images

from the detective school's file, from Granddad Ian's notebook of witness statements, and an assortment of photos that Dash projected onto the screen with his multifunction EyeNet device.

When Agatha described the ridiculous visions reported to her grandfather during the interviews, the audience chuckled at each explanation.

"What about the gunshot I heard?" shouted someone. "Can you explain that?"

A photo of the little girl appeared on the screen. She was holding a balloon and standing under an imposing halberd. Her eyelids were drooping.

Chandler moved between the tables to the exact same spot, and picked up a deflated balloon from the floor.

"When she got sleepy and let the balloon slip out of her hand, it hit the point of the halberd, and burst, sounding just like . . . a gunshot!" Agatha smiled.

Her explanation was met with a round of applause and she took a deep breath. The hardest part was just beginning.

"Now, ladies and gentlemen," she stated. "It's time to explain how you all fell asleep. There's a certain powder that brings on a near-instantaneous sleep just by coming in contact with the skin, and all of you touched an object that was covered in it."

A chorus of voices filled the room, some angry, some frightened, some curious. Questions

of every kind rained down at once.

Agatha waited for silence before she continued. "Given the timing," she began in the tone of an expert detective, "the only people who could have handled this substance are sitting right in the front row: the organizers of this event. Each of them has a motivation to possess the king of Scotland's sword."

"What are you saying?" roared Snodgrass. His face looked red enough to burst into flames.

"She's making this up!" said Professor Cunningham. "There must be a logical explanation."

Director MacKenzie was shaking like a leaf, while the Earl of Duncan tugged at his kilt, affronted. "What a shameful accusation! An insult to my noble house!"

Chandler stepped forward, with the two police officers flanking him, just in case.

Agatha asked the audience to please remain

calm. This was the moment of truth. "After careful analysis, my colleagues and I have discovered that there is only one object that each of you touched as you entered," she continued.

She turned around to pick up the evidence, sealed in a ziplock bag. She held it up to the audience. "It's the exhibition program, which you were each given at the castle entrance at eight fifteen this morning!"

Guests exclaimed in astonishment, hurling insults at the organizing committee.

"But we were all asleep, too!" protested Director MacKenzie over the chaos. "Don't pay attention to this silly nonsense!"

Agatha smiled, concluding her speech. "Three of you were asleep, but one of you stayed awake and stole the king of Scotland's sword!"

She gestured to Dash and an unmistakable image appeared on the screen: Professor Cunningham, smiling as he handed programs to

the guests. He was wearing a pair of white silk gloves.

The young antiques dealer jumped up and tried to escape, but the policemen tackled him instantly, each taking him by one arm. As they handcuffed him, the alarmed guests made so much noise that Chandler ushered them all to the door, using his significant powers of persuasion.

Director MacKenzie, the Earl of Duncan, and Snodgrass followed them, doing their best to appease their guests with kind words and apologies.

The curtain came down on the arms hall at Dunnottar Castle.

Agatha and Dash couldn't believe they had caught the culprit of the craziest theft they could remember.

But it wouldn't be over until they had tracked down the king of Scotland's sword.

"Blasted meddlers!" Professor Cunningham

hissed. "My plan was perfect, and you amateurs ruined everything! I can't understand how you figured it out with all the false clues I set up to throw you off track . . ."

Agatha asked the policemen to search him, then said, "Dear Professor, it was the very excess of clues that led us to you, including throwing Ms. Ross's purse into that well. You took advantage of the time she spent making coffee, then sent her out to look for the permits just before the exhibition opened, so she'd come back and find you asleep with the others."

"Then we scanned all the objects you scattered around the castle, and didn't find one single fingerprint," explained Dash. "Your fine silk gloves implicated you twice!"

The officers emptied the prisoner's pockets and placed everything on the table. There was a snakeskin wallet, some loose change, and a bunch of car keys.

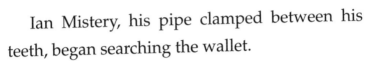

Ian Mistery, his pipe clamped between his teeth, began searching the wallet.

Professor Cunningham burst out laughing. "Search all you like, but you'll never find out where I hid the sword," he hissed. "It's already on its way to my secret buyer's private collection!"

Dash looked at Agatha, anxious. If they didn't recover the sword, he would fail his exam!

Agatha advanced on the young antiques dealer. "That's a beautiful ring, Professor Cunningham," she flattered him, observing his hands in the handcuffs. "But it doesn't quite go with your fine tailored outfit!"

Dash couldn't believe his ears. What was Agatha doing, complimenting this man? Was she trying to get the location of the sword?

Suddenly he understood where his cousin was going. "Officers, would you please remove his ring for me?" he asked.

Professor Cunningham tried to wriggle away,

but the two policemen kept hold of him and pulled the large ring from his finger. Scrutinizing it carefully, Dash discovered a tiny electronic device on the inside. "Agatha, there's a GPS receiver here!" he exclaimed. "What do you think it's for?"

She thought for a moment, staring out the castle window, as if reconstructing the scene of the crime. "I've got it!" she exclaimed suddenly. "It's so simple!"

Dash, Granddad Ian, and Chandler stared at her. So did the police.

"Why would the professor need a GPS receiver if the sword were hidden somewhere in the castle?" she asked. "And if he passed it off to an accomplice, why would he need to be able to track it?"

"You little know-it-all!" snapped Professor Cunningham, attempting to struggle again. "Hold your tongue!"

Agatha pointed her finger at the wall overlooking the cliff. "This is the way it went," she stated. "The professor took the sword from the display cabinet, secured it to a flotation device equipped with a GPS signal, then threw the whole thing, including his tainted gloves, over that wall!"

Dash's eyes bulged. "Are you serious? He threw the king of Scotland's sword off a cliff into the North Sea?"

Agatha shrugged. "What's the matter, dear cousin?" she asked calmly. "Just plug that GPS into your EyeNet and we'll know exactly where it is!"

Professor Cunningham's furious shouts were all the proof they needed that Agatha had indeed solved the mystery.

Mystery Solved...

*T*he next morning, Director MacKenzie came to congratulate Agatha and her companions for solving the case, assuring them that he'd already informed Eye International of the good news.

Granddad Ian suggested they continue their trip toward the Orkney Islands, off the northern tip of Scotland, where strong ocean currents had pulled the inflatable raft with the sword.

Dash and Agatha were delighted.

The hot-air balloon trip passed quickly, with breathtaking views of the coastline. Finally the *Mistery Balloon* landed at Stenness, a village on Orkney's main island, just as the police were

Mystery Solved . . .

hauling the king of Scotland's sword off the kelp-strewn beach.

The precious claymore was wrapped in a classic orange life jacket.

There were lots of curious onlookers, but the authorities weren't allowing anyone to get close.

Dash was disappointed. "Don't they know we're the people who tracked it here? I'd like to get a look at that thing!"

"Sorry, cousin. Looks like you'll have to wait for the next exhibition!" said Agatha.

Watson agreed with a loud meow.

They all started to laugh, but were interrupted by the piercing ring of Dash's EyeNet.

"Aren't you going to answer that?" asked Agatha, noticing that her cousin was staring at it in terror.

"Uh-oh, what if it's Dorothy?" he said, shuffling his feet. "What do I say to her? I'm a wreck when it comes to that heart stuff . . ."

His grandfather smiled. "So you can face dangerous criminals, but you're afraid of a pretty girl?"

Agatha took advantage of Dash's distraction to press a button on the EyeNet, stopping its incessant ringing.

A message appeared on the screen:

CONGRATULATIONS ON YOUR GOOD WORK, AGENT DM14! YOU PASSED YOUR EXAM WITH FLYING COLORS AND EARNED AN EXTRA WEEK OF VACATION. EXCEPT FROM MISSIONS.

Dash stared at the screen with eyes full of joy.

"Come on, vacation boy. Let's take a walk!" Agatha suggested. Dash, Chandler, and Granddad Ian fell into step behind her, trailed by a bounding Watson.

"Do you know how lucky we are?" said Agatha. "There are ancient, megalithic stones right here in Stenness. Look at that one there, it's over sixteen feet tall!"

The group gathered around a tall boulder, one of a large circle of standing stones that reminded them all of Stonehenge.

Agatha, always eager to learn something new, stopped to study the stones' ancient runes. While she made notes in her notebook, Granddad Ian and Chandler chattered about the beautiful countryside.

Dash had been silent for a long time, staring down at his feet. Suddenly he grabbed Agatha's shoulder. "I need help!" he cried, agitated. "I don't know what to do!"

"What's the matter, dear cousin?"

He shook his head, embarrassed. "I promised Dorothy I'd call her, but I don't have a clue what to say!"

"What's Dorothy like?" asked Agatha.

"She's really cool. Funny, smart, and, um, totally gorgeous." Dash flushed bright red. "Her real name is Aileen," he explained. "When we were little, everyone called her 'Dorothy' because she always dressed like the girl from *The Wizard of Oz*, you know . . . blue pinafore, ruby slippers . . ."

Agatha thought it over. "Sounds to me like she's a romantic, dreamy sort of girl," she mused. "If you ask me, you should flirt with her, old-school."

"What do you mean?" Dash looked completely stressed, massaging his forehead as if he had the world's biggest headache.

"Skip the technology. No phone calls, no email, no texting," said Agatha. "Try surprising your sweetheart with a handwritten postcard from the Orkney Islands . . . You'll see, it'll make her think you're really interesting."

"You really think that'll work on Dorothy?"

"I'm positive!" said Agatha. "Girls love it when guys make an effort." Then she added, "And stop calling her 'Dorothy.' Her name is Aileen!"

"You're right, I need to remember!" Dash nodded.

He ran to a nearby souvenir shop and came

back with a postcard depicting the beautiful landscape in front of them. "What should I write?" he asked, panting.

"Sit down, contemplate the view, and look for words that come right from your heart. Just tell

her what you're looking at—and that you wish she could see it, too."

He followed her instructions to the letter. Ten minutes later, he stood up, finished.

"Can you please read it?" he asked. "I don't think I'm much of a writer."

Agatha turned away. "Are you kidding me? Some things are private. Go mail that postcard. I

don't want to know anything about it!"

"You don't know what you're missing," he joked, feeling cheerful again.

He ran back to the shop and dropped the postcard into the mailbox. "I'll conquer your heart, Aileen," he whispered, blissfully imagining their next candlelit meal.

Too bad he'd forgotten to put on a stamp . . .

Agatha
Girl of Mystery

Agatha's Next Mystery:
The Heist at Niagara Falls

The Investigation Begins...

High above the streets of London, the orange rays of a spectacular sunset blazed through a tangle of high-tech wires and houseplants into Dashiell Mistery's penthouse atop Baker Palace. The blinding light hid the mess in the living room as its sole occupant dedicated himself to doing what he did best: making an even bigger mess.

Tall and lanky, with black hair that always flopped over his forehead, fourteen-year-old Dash was multitasking on seven computers at once: blaring rock music from iTunes, talking to friends on chat, opening a dozen web pages simultaneously, and—most important of all—

installing new software for his EyeNet, the state-of-the-art device given to students at the detective school he attended.

Nearly hidden by pizza boxes and socks, the precious titanium instrument vibrated with high-speed downloads. Every so often, Dash checked to make sure that it was updating smoothly. The new programs would allow him to view microfilm from anywhere in the world, connect wirelessly to other EyeNets, and track the movement of satellites in real time. The aspiring detective couldn't wait to try out these exciting new features during an investigation.

"Watch your back, Sherlock Holmes," he said with a snicker. "Soon I'll be the most famous detective in all of London!"

Satisfied, he put his feet up on the desk and leaned way back, balancing on the rear wheels of his chair. This proved to be a risky move. A moment later, the chair's plastic joints gave way with a *CRACK*! and Dash fell backward onto the dusty carpet, dragging a mess of cables, computers, and monitors with him. "What a wipeout!" he groaned, struggling to free himself from the tangle of wires. Fortunately, his mother was out, so there were no witnesses . . . He didn't exactly look like the best detective in London!

At that very moment, Dash spotted a silhouette hidden behind the jasmine plants on the terrace. Squinting into the sunset, he could make out a man with a brown peaked cap and a digital camera hiding his face.

The camera flashed ten times in rapid succession, and then the mysterious man took off at high speed.

"Hey! Cut it out!" Dash yelled. "Who gave you permission to . . . to—Oh no!" His voice caught in his throat. Who would want to immortalize such an embarrassing moment?

There was only one possibility, and it was

a doozy: His school must have him under surveillance. And Eye International Detective Academy was staffed by the most elite experts in the field!

Dash jumped up, grabbed his EyeNet, and raced onto the terrace. He looked down the emergency stairs. The man in the brown hat was already a full flight below. There was no time to lose!

Stay calm, he told himself. *Follow procedure.*

Last month, he'd participated in a Tracking and Diversion course taught by Professor MP37, and he had learned the three fundamental rules of shadowing someone.

First rule: *Never attract attention.*

Second rule: *Never lose sight of your target.*

Third rule . . .

Um . . . Dash couldn't remember it. "I need to study the manual more," he groaned. "My cousin Agatha can store every detail in her famous memory drawers!"

He raced down the stairs to the floor below, just in time to see the elevator doors close. The glowing numbers indicated that it was heading straight to the ground floor.

Dash bit his lip. What was he going to do now?

"The stairs!" he exclaimed, snapping his fingers. He raced down fifteen flights at breakneck speed and arrived in the lobby of Baker Palace, panting and sweating. "Did a man with a brown hat and camera go out this way?" he gasped to the doorman.

The elderly man seemed surprised. "Do you mean Mr. Marlowe?" he replied in a quavering voice. "Well, now, I think he just left . . ."

Dash rolled his eyes and shot out the front door like lightning.

He couldn't believe it!

Mr. Marlowe was his whiny neighbor . . . Who would ever have suspected that he could be a spy from Eye International? Dash figured he'd better catch up with Mr. Marlowe fast, tell him that his cover was blown, and beg him to delete the embarrassing photos!

Remembering his moves from Tracking and Diversion class, he scanned the street like a bird of prey and spied a brown hat near a sign for the Underground. Mr. Marlowe walked briskly, checking his watch, as though he were late for an appointment. Apparently, he had not realized that Dash was hot on his trail.

"I'll get you, you nosy meddler!" growled the boy.

They turned one corner after another, heading toward deserted backstreets. Finally, Mr. Marlowe slipped into The King's Head, one of the most popular pubs in central London. Dash stopped to consider his next move. What *was* that third rule of shadowing? Was he supposed to sneak inside, or wait for his target to reemerge?

After a brief hesitation, he decided to stroll slowly past the pub window to check out Mr. Marlowe's whereabouts. Dash spotted him at the bar, conferring with a woman in a blonde wig, a floor-length gray coat, and an oversize pair of dark sunglasses. The disguise made her features unrecognizable; surely she must be an Eye International agent.

"He must be passing her the camera!" Dash shuddered, remembering his disastrous fall. "I'll be expelled for being a klutz!"

Suddenly the woman looked right at the window, and Dash ducked behind a rusty pipe to avoid being seen. At that precise moment, the third rule of shadowing popped into his mind: *Be careful you don't fall into a trap.*

"They've lured me here for some reason!" he muttered, running a hand through his hair. "I have to get out of here right away!"

As he walked down the street, whistling and

doing his best to look carefree, Mr. Marlowe and his accomplice came out of the pub. Dash immediately dived into a Dumpster, covering himself with disgusting garbage bags. The possibility that he'd be discovered made him uneasy. "No, no, no!" he begged quietly, as he peeked out from under the lid. "I don't want to be expelled!"

Fortunately, the Eye International agents disappeared around the corner. Dash gave a sigh of relief and clambered out of the Dumpster.

"Ha! I was put to the test," he rejoiced, wiping slime off his clothes. "But I passed with flying colors!"

He barely had time to finish his sentence when his EyeNet started to beep. Dash thought it must be the Tracking and Diversion teacher calling to congratulate him, but a message lit up the screen. His face went pale. "An urgent mission at Niagara Falls!?" he hissed. "And here

I am, covered with garbage!"

He scraped a banana peel off his sleeve and almost flew down the steps to the Underground. There was just one thing he knew for certain: Without the help of his brilliant cousin Agatha Mistery, he would be lost!